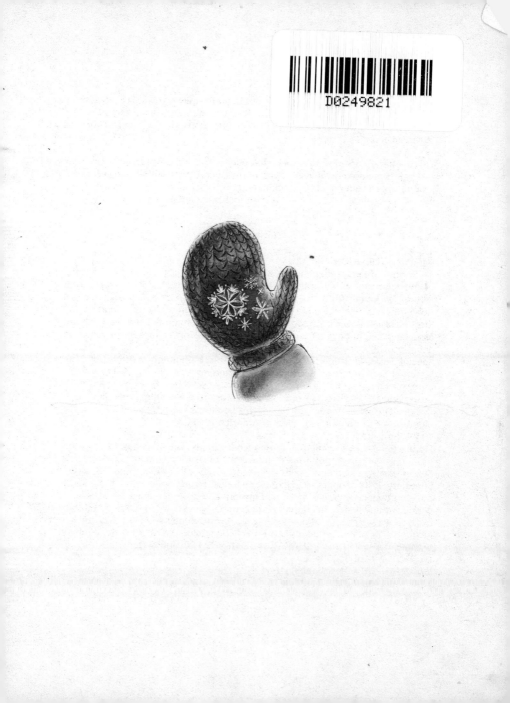

 LITTLE SIMON

An imprint of Simon & Schuster Children's Publishing Division • 1230 Avenue of the Americas, New York, New York 10020 • First Little Simon paperback edition December 2015 • Copyright © 2015 by Simon & Schuster, Inc. All rights reserved, including the right of reproduction in whole or in part in any form. LITTLE SIMON is a registered trademark of Simon & Schuster, Inc., and associated colophon is a trademark of Simon & Schuster, Inc. For information about special discounts for bulk purchases, please contact Simon & Schuster Special Sales at 1-866-506-1949 or business@simonandschuster.com. The Simon & Schuster Speakers Bureau can bring authors to your live event. For more information or to book an event contact the Simon & Schuster Speakers Bureau at 1-866-248-3049 or visit our website at www.simonspeakers.com. Designed by Laura Roode. The text of this book was set in Usherwood. Manufactured in the United States of America 1015 FFG
10 9 8 7 6 5 4 3 2 1
Library of Congress Cataloging-in-Publication Data   Green, Poppy. Winter's no time to sleep! / by Poppy Green ; illustrated by Jennifer A. Bell. — First Little Simon paperback edition. pages cm. — (The adventures of Sophie Mouse ; 6) Summary: While Sophie Mouse and her forest friends are playing in the snow one day, they accidentally wake a hibernating hedgehog named Pippa, who is a little grumpy at first, but Sophie, Hattie, and Owen show her all the fun things to do in wintertime. [1. Mice—Fiction. 2. Forest animals—Fiction. 3. Winter—Fiction.] I. Bell, Jennifer (Jennifer A.), 1977- illustrator. II. Title. III. Title: Winter's no time to sleep! PZ7.G82616Wi 2015 [Fic]—dc23 2015006941
ISBN 978-1-4814-4200-8 (hc)
ISBN 978-1-4814-4199-5 (pbk)
ISBN 978-1-4814-4201-5 (eBook)

the adventures of
SOPHIE MOUSE

6

winter's No Time to sleep!
WITHDRAWN

By Poppy Green • Illustrated by Jennifer A. Bell

LITTLE SIMON
New York London Toronto Sydney New Delhi

Contents

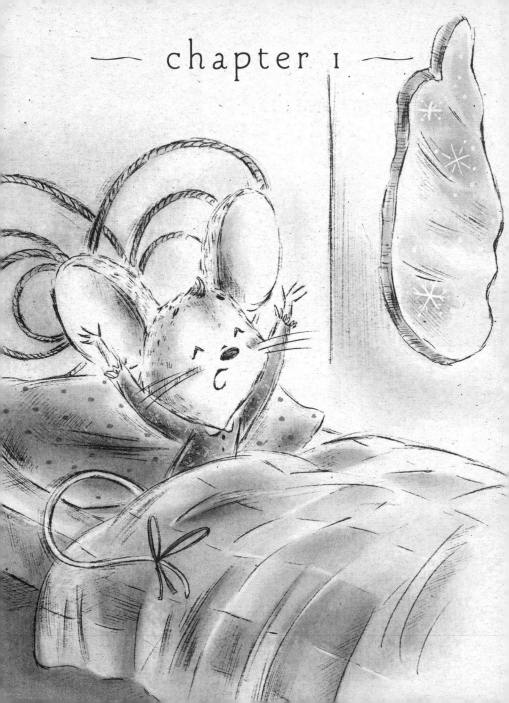

winter white

Sophie yawned and sat up in her bed. The early morning light glowed through her window. She squinted and blinked hard.

Sophie rubbed her eyes. She gasped. *Is that what I think it is?* she wondered excitedly. Her vision cleared. White flakes drifted past her window. Snow! It was snowing!

Sophie leaped out of bed. She pressed her nose and whiskers against the frosty window. Outside, a blanket of white covered the sleeping forest.

"A snow day!" Sophie squeaked. "At last!" It was the first snowfall since winter had come. Her class at Silverlake Elementary had been on winter break for a week. But now the wintertime fun could really begin!

Still in her pajamas, Sophie tiptoed downstairs. She went to the front door and pulled it open. A little pile of snow fell onto the floor.

Sophie looked around. The forest was a glistening winter wonderland!

Sophie breathed in the crisp air. Her ears perked up, listening. It was so quiet and still—except for clumps of snow softly falling from trees. Sophie imagined all the animals tucked away in their cozy homes.

"You're up early," said a voice behind her. Sophie turned. Her dad, George Mouse, was coming downstairs. "I can't imagine why," he added with a smile. "How about we make blueberry pancakes and some rhubarb tea for everyone?"

Sophie nodded and joined her dad in the kitchen. They mixed up some pancake batter. Mr. Mouse got a jar of preserved blueberries from the root cellar. Sophie stirred them into the batter.

Her dad heated a pan. It sizzled as he dropped in blobs of batter. He spooned two small blobs next to a larger one. The batter ran together to make . . .

"A mouse!" Sophie cried. "Can I try one?" She loved to draw and paint. And even making pancakes was art to her!

George Mouse handed her the spoon. Sophie made three blobs stacked on top of one another. Onto the last blob, she added two tiny drops.

"Aha!" said George Mouse. "A *snow* mouse!"

Before long, the smell of pancakes lured Sophie's mom and brother downstairs.

"Surprise!" Sophie cried when she saw Lily Mouse and Winston. "Sit down. Breakfast is ready!"

"Yippee!" Winston cried as the Mouse family sat down to warm pancakes and hot tea. Sophie

took her seat by the window. She reached for the syrup and gazed outside. The snow sure was piling up!

I bet it'll be up to the tops of my boots, Sophie thought. Her mind swirled with snowy ideas. *I can make snow angels! And snow mice! And snow forts! But first I want to go sledding at Hickory Hill! I'll pick up Hattie and Owen and we can—*

"Sophie?" Her mother's voice interrupted her snowdream. "Sophie! Your pancakes!"

Sophie looked down. Her plate was almost overflowing with syrup.

"Oops!" Sophie cried. She put down

the syrup jug. "I guess I was thinking about something else."

Lily Mouse smiled. "I guess so!"

chapter 2

Snow Buddies

Sophie got ready to go outside. She pulled on her warmest woolen leggings. She laced up her boots.

"I'll be at the bakery," Mrs. Mouse said. She owned the only bakery in Pine Needle Grove. "Folks still need their bread. Even in snow!"

George Mouse added, "But I'll be here, Sophie. Come home when your toes get cold." Sophie's dad was an architect. He was going to sketch at his desk—between snowball fights with Winston, of course.

"Okay!" said Sophie. She bundled up in her warmest winter jacket.

"Oh!" said Lily Mouse. "I almost forgot!" She got her tote bag. She pulled out a purple bundle, tied with a ribbon.

Then she handed it to Sophie. "I've been knitting when business is slow," she explained. "I finished it yesterday."

Sophie untied the ribbon. The bundle unfurled into a long purple scarf. "It's so beautiful!" Sophie exclaimed. She wrapped it around her neck. "And so warm and soft!" She gave her mom a big hug. "I love it!" cried Sophie. "I'm never taking it off. Thank you, Mom."

"You're welcome," Mrs. Mouse replied with

a smile. "Now go have fun!"

So Sophie tromped off. The snow crunched under her feet. She headed straight for her best friend Hattie Frog's house. The friends *always* played outside on the first snow day of the year.

But it was still early. *I wonder if Hattie's up yet,* Sophie thought. She reached the Frog family's house on the bank of the stream. The window shutters were closed. Sophie decided to knock quietly in case they were still asleep. She raised her hand to the door.

But before she could knock, it swung wide open. And there was Hattie, dressed and ready.

"What took you so long?" Hattie teased Sophie. "I've been ready since sunrise!"

Sophie laughed. "Sledding at Hickory Hill?" she suggested. "We could get Owen on the way."

"Yeah!" Hattie replied. She said good-bye to her

mom and dad. Then the two friends set off toward town. They walked all the way to the other side of town, where Owen's house was. In the warm months, the Snake family lived in a house nestled in a bunch of lily plants. But as the cold came on, the leaves dried up. So Owen's family moved into tunnels *beneath* their house. Sophie and Hattie had to dig a little in the snow to find the

door. Sophie knocked.

The door opened a crack. Mrs. Snake peeked out. When she saw Sophie and Hattie, she flung it open wide. "Hello! Look at you, snow bunnies . . . I mean snow mouse and frog!"

Owen peeked around his mom.

"Sophie! Hattie!" he exclaimed.

"Want to come sledding?" Sophie asked excitedly.

Owen beamed. He looked at his mom for an okay. She nodded and smiled.

In a flash, Owen zipped out the door. He squeezed between Sophie and Hattie. He slithered away fast, leaving a ripple pattern in the snow.

"Come on!" Owen called back to them. "Last one to Hickory Hill is a stinky mushroom!"

chapter 3

Hickory Hill

Sophie and Hattie ran to catch up with Owen. They walked back through town and past Forget-Me-Not Lake. It was frozen solid. A big section of ice had been swept clear of snow. Sophie could see scratches on it.

"Someone's been skating," Sophie pointed out.

"We could do that too!" said Owen.

Hattie nodded. "But sledding first. Look!" she said as she pointed toward some trees with white trunks. "Birches! Maybe we can find some bark for sleds."

Birch bark was perfect for sleds. Maple bark was too bumpy. Oak was even bumpier. But birch bark was smooth and thin—flexible but strong. And sometimes it came off in a big sheet.

Hattie found a
fallen birch branch
in the snow.
She grasped
a piece of bark
that was peeling
up. She pulled
slowly . . . carefully . . .
until it came loose.

"Big enough?" Hattie
asked. "If we go one at
a time?"

Sophie and Owen
nodded. "Good job,
Hattie!" cried Sophie.
"You get the first ride!"

Working together, they carried
their birch-bark sled down the path.
Soon they came out of the woods.
There was Hickory Hill! It was big and
wide, and covered with untracked
snow.

They climbed up to the top. Hattie knelt on the sled. She grabbed the front and curled it up over her knees.

Sophie put a hand on Hattie's back. "Ready? Set? Hold on tight!" She gave Hattie a big push.

"Whoo-hooooooo!" Hattie's voice

trailed off as she sped away.

A few minutes later, Hattie ran the sled back up the hill. "That was *so* fun!" she cried. "Who's next?"

"You go, Owen!" said Sophie. So Owen coiled up on the sled. Sophie and Hattie gave him a push.

"Aaaaaaaaaah!" Owen called the whole way down. He slid a few yards farther than Hattie had.

Owen wriggled his way back up the hill. It was Sophie's turn. "Give me a really, *really* big push," she told her friends.

"You asked for it!" said Owen.

Hattie started jogging as she pushed Sophie. Owen slithered next to her, pushing his head against Sophie's back. They pushed and pushed until Sophie rocketed away.

The air ruffled Sophie's fur. Snow sprayed into her eyes. The sled raced down the track Hattie and Owen had packed down. Sophie leaned forward, trying to go faster!

She got to the bottom of the hill. And the sled kept going! It flew past the spots where Hattie and Owen had stopped.

Oh no! thought Sophie. She was headed right for the bushes!

chapter 4

Wake-Up Call

Sophie—and the sled—plunged into the underbrush and came to a stop. Sophie could hear her friends running down the hill.

"Sophie!" Owen called out. "Are you okay?"

He and Hattie arrived breathless. Hattie offered Sophie a hand. Sophie stood up and shook the snow off

her leggings. She caught her breath.
"That was the best ride ever!" she
exclaimed, laughing and still breath-
ing in deep gulps.

Just then, Sophie heard a squeak.
She looked at Hattie and Owen. They
froze, listening. They'd heard it too.

There was another squeak. And another.

Sophie leaned toward the bushes. It was coming from in there!

"Uh . . . hello?" Owen called.

For a long moment, there was no reply. Then a little voice squeaked, "Hello."

The friends looked at one another. *Who was that?*

Sophie peered into the brush. But she couldn't see much. "I'm going in," she said.

"Wait!" cried Hattie. "You don't know what's in there."

Sophie smiled. Hattie was always so careful. But Sophie wasn't worried. "Scary things don't *usually* have squeaky voices."

Hattie still didn't look so sure.

"Then let's go in together," she said.

So Sophie, Hattie, and Owen inched into the thick underbrush. They took turns holding branches aside to let the others go through. Sheltered by the branches and trees overhead, the ground was free of snow.

Sophie stopped. Hattie and Owen did too. A big mound of dry leaves and grass blocked their way.

As they started to walk around one side, they saw it. It was an opening—a door in the mound. And poking out was a little head. It was covered in spiky fur and had a tiny brown nose.

The animal stepped out of the doorway. It was a hedgehog!

"Oh, hi!" Sophie said.

"Shhhhhh," the hedgehog whispered. She yawned, turned, and shuffled back into her nest.

Sophie looked at Hattie and Owen. "I think we scared her," she said.

Hattie still looked nervous. She stayed behind Sophie and peeked over her shoulder. But Owen leaned toward the door of the nest. "Sorry," he whispered. "We didn't mean to bother you."

Just then, the hedgehog reappeared, startling Owen. Now she was wearing a purple sweater, green pants, and a red scarf. She motioned to them to follow her. She led them away from the nest and then turned around.

"Hi," she mumbled sleepily. "I'm Pippa. Didn't mean to be rude." She rubbed her eyes. "I just didn't want

to wake my brothers and sisters."

Sophie and Owen introduced themselves too. "And this is Hattie," Owen added. Hattie was still being a little shy.

"Is your family nocturnal?" Sophie asked Pippa. She knew that some

animals slept during the day and were awake at night.

Pippa nodded. "We *are* nocturnal. But we hibernate, too. So we sleep through most of the winter." She gave a big yawn.

Hattie came out from behind

Sophie. She seemed to realize Pippa
wasn't scary. "So why aren't *you*
sleeping?" Hattie asked.

Pippa sighed. "I should be, but a
loud noise woke me up. I think the
brush even shook a little."

Sophie was embarrassed. "Sorry.
That was me crashing my sled."

"Oh," said Pippa, nodding her head. "Wait. What's a sled?"

Owen laughed. "You know. For riding in the snow?"

"Oh," said Pippa, nodding again. "I've heard of snow. But I've never seen it."

Sophie was shocked.

Pippa had *never* seen snow?

chapter 5

Pippa's First Snow Day

Then Sophie realized: "You're always asleep in the winter!"

"Ohhh," said Owen and Hattie, getting it.

Sophie gasped. "Do you *want* to see some snow?" she asked. "Right now?"

Suddenly, Pippa's eyes opened wide. She nodded excitedly. Sophie

led the way. Hattie, Owen, and Pippa
followed to the edge of the underbrush. Pippa peeked out.

At first, she squinted in the light.
But slowly her eyes got used to it. She
looked up, down, and all around.

"Wow," she said in awe. "It's

beautiful! And it's just . . . frozen water?"

Sophie picked up a clump of snow. She spread it out in her hand. "See each little ice crystal? They're snowflakes!"

Pippa studied the snowflakes. Then she gazed out at the snow-covered hill. "Imagine how many snowflakes it takes to make . . . all this!" Pippa said.

"I've never really thought about that before!" Sophie said to Pippa. It *was* amazing!

Pippa smiled. "You know what?" she said. "Suddenly I don't feel so tired."

"Well, since you're awake," said
Owen, "do you want to play with us?"

Sophie added, "There are *lots* of
fun things to do in the wintertime!"

Hattie pulled a pair of earmuffs
from her coat pocket. "And you

could borrow these," she said. Hattie
adjusted them to fit Pippa's head.

Pippa beamed. "Thank you!" she
said. "So . . . what should we do
first?"

"How about some more sledding?"
Sophie suggested.

Pippa was nervous to try it. She watched Sophie, Hattie, and Owen take their turns. "Watch out for the underbrush!" Pippa teased just before Sophie went.

Sophie laughed. "No more crashes today!" she said.

Finally, the friends got Pippa to take a ride. "The snow is nice and soft," Owen told her. "Even if you fall off, you'll be fine."

They gave Pippa a gentle push.

She picked up speed and slid away. Pippa didn't whoop or cheer on her way down. Sophie watched, worrying. Did she hate it? Sophie couldn't tell! Not until after Pippa had come to a stop.

Suddenly there came a big "Yahoooooo!" from the bottom of the hill. It was so loud it echoed off the trees.

Sophie laughed. "Well, I think she likes it!"

Next, they built a snow animal on top of the hill. They thought about building a snow snake, a snow frog,

or a snow hedgehog. In the end,
they thought a snow mouse would
be easiest.

They showed Pippa how to roll
snow into balls. They stacked them
up. Then they found small sticks to
use as whiskers.

Hattie dug in the snow looking for pebbles for eyes. Sophie added two snowballs on top for ears.

She was adding a few more items

to the snow mouse when—*whomp!* Something cold hit the back of her neck. A snowball!

She whirled around. Owen was giggling—and making another snow-ball with his tail!

Sophie scooped up some snow.
She chased Owen down the hill.
"Snowball fight!" the animals cried.

chapter 6

Snow Much Fun!

The four friends divided up into teams: Owen and Pippa versus Sophie and Hattie. Then, at the edge of the woods, the snowball fight began!

Owen's secret weapon was his tail. Using it, he could fling the snowballs so far!

But Sophie's secret weapon was Hattie. Always practical, she started

building a snow wall. She and Sophie hid behind it. While Sophie threw snowballs, Hattie made the wall bigger and wider. Owen and Pippa threw tons of snowballs. But they were all hitting the wall.

"Sneak attack!" cried Owen. He and Pippa ran up to the wall and jumped on top of it. The soft wall crumbled.

Everyone laughed and flopped down into the snow.

They lay there, resting, gazing up at the wintry sky. Sophie took a scoop of fresh snow. She ate it like a snow cone.

"So how come you don't go to

Silverlake Elementary?" Sophie asked
Pippa.

"My mom homeschools us," Pippa
replied.

Owen added, "Plus, you live pretty

far from the schoolhouse. It would be a long walk."

"Do you ever get bored—not going to school?" Hattie asked.

Pippa shook her head. "No. I have five brothers and sisters! We play

a lot. And we have playdates with friends. There are lots of other animals on Hickory Hill!"

Pippa asked them about school. Sophie described their teacher, Mrs. Wise. Then Hattie listed all their classmates. Owen talked about the games they played at recess when the weather was warm.

"But we know some snow games, too," Hattie told Pippa. "Like snow hide-and-seek! Whoever's 'it' tries to find the hiders by following tracks in the snow. But the hiders try to make their tracks confusing and hard to follow."

Pippa's eyes lit up. "That sounds so fun!" she said. "Can we play? Now?"

The others agreed. One by one, they stood up. They shook off the snow. Suddenly Owen laughed. He pointed at the snow they had been lying in.

Side by side, there were four very different imprints. It was easy to see who had made each one!

Starting their game, the friends made their way into the woods. There were lots of good places to hide.

Owen was "it." He covered his eyes and counted. Sophie, Hattie, and Pippa ran off to hide.

chapter 7

Slip-Sliding Away

The friends took turns being "it." When it was Sophie's turn, she found Owen first. She found Pippa next. But as hard as she tried she could not find Hattie—not even with Owen's and Pippa's help!

Finally, Sophie called, "Come out, come out, wherever you are!"

Hattie peeked out from the

branches of a fir tree. "Here I am!"

"Wow!" said Sophie. "Good hiding, Hattie. We've been looking for you forever!"

Hattie smiled proudly. She had made tracks leading to a hollow log. From there, she'd hopped straight up into the tree. The fir needles had kept her hidden as she crouched on the branch.

"What should we do next?" Owen asked. They had played many rounds of snow hide-and-seek. "Ice skating?"

"Yeah!" cried Sophie, remembering how frozen Forget-Me-Not Lake was.

"Um, *ice skating*?" said Pippa uncertainly.

Hattie patted her on the back. "Don't worry! You'll *love* it!"

The friends tromped through the woods. Soon they were standing on the bank of the lake. Pippa cautiously put her foot onto the ice. "Cool!" she exclaimed. "I've never seen it like this!"

Sophie, Owen, and Hattie found some icicles dangling from a craggy rock. Sophie snapped two of them off.

"These will be your skates!" Sophie told Pippa. "Watch!"

Gently, Sophie scraped the icicle along the rock. She did it again and again, shaving the icicle down. Soon it had a sharp edge on one side.

Sophie, Hattie, and Owen quickly made their own skates too. Then they found some bendy pine twigs. They used them to tie the icicles to their feet. They helped Pippa put hers on.

Then all four friends teetered onto the ice.

"Whoa!" Pippa cried, slipping a little. She grabbed onto Sophie for balance. Sophie skated backward, holding Pippa's hands. At first, Pippa was walking on the ice. But Sophie encouraged her to glide. "Watch Hattie. See how she pushes off with one foot and glides?"

Pippa watched Hattie. She tried it herself. The first few times, she almost fell down. But she kept trying. Each time, she glided a little farther.

Then Pippa let go of Sophie's

hands. She pushed off once, twice.
She glided, finding her balance. Then
she did it all over again.

Pippa was skating!

"Way to go, Pippa!" Sophie called
out after her. "You've got it!"

Hattie and Owen skated up to

Pippa. They clapped and cheered.

Sophie did a few figure eights. She practiced her jumps and spins. Then she took a rest. An icy wind blew across the lake. Sophie shivered. She reached up to tighten her scarf around her neck.

But her scarf wasn't there.

Sophie looked down. Had it just fallen off? She looked all around her on the ice. No scarf.

She skated over to the rock where they'd made the skates. No scarf.

Sophie looked along the bank of the lake. She couldn't find it anywhere.

Oh no! thought Sophie. *My special scarf from Mom is lost!*

chapter 8

The Scarf
Search

Hattie came over to Sophie. "What's the matter?" she asked.

Sophie explained that she'd lost her scarf. "My mom knit it for me," she said. Tears welled up in her eyes. "She gave it to me this morning."

"Don't worry," said Owen. "We'll help you find it!"

But Sophie was still worried. "I'vc

looked around. It's not here," she told her friends.

Hattie gave Sophie a squeeze. "Maybe you dropped it on the way," she said. "It's okay. We'll retrace our steps. We'll look in *all* the places we've been today."

Pippa nodded. "It's a purple scarf, right? I remember it! You were wearing it when I met you. Definitely."

Hattie clapped. "That's a clue! So Sophie lost the scarf sometime *after* we met Pippa. And *before* we got to the lake."

Sophie wiped her eyes and tried to smile.

They all took off their skates. Then they headed

back toward Hickory Hill. The snow came in handy. They could follow their tracks to go back exactly the way they'd come.

They went slowly. They looked

up, down, and all around. But they
didn't find the scarf.

Soon they came to a clearing.
"This is where we played snow hide-
and-seek," Owen pointed out.

Sophie checked all the places she had hidden. The others looked around on the ground. Hattie gently kicked at the snow, in case the scarf had gotten covered. But there was no scarf.

They continued on and came out of the woods. There in front of them were the imprints they'd made by lying in the snow.

"I remember lying here eating snow," Sophie said. "But I can't remember if I had my scarf!"

They looked all around but found nothing.

Sophie frowned. "We're almost back at Pippa's house," she said. "We're running out of places to look."

But Hattie pointed over Sophie's shoulder. "Don't forget our snowball fight!" she said. "There's our snow wall. Or what's left of it."

Full of fresh hope, Sophie scurried over. She *did* remember something about the last time she saw her scarf . . . and a snowball?

Did I drop it during the snowball fight? she thought. She dug around the wrecked wall.

There was nothing there but snow.

So the friends climbed up Hickory Hill, looking all around. Sophie's shoulders slumped. Sledding was the first thing they'd done with Pippa. *If my scarf isn't here on the hill . . . then we won't find it, after all.*

Up ahead, Pippa reached the crest of the hill. She stopped, pointing at something in front of her. But it was out of Sophie's line of sight.

"Look!" Pippa shouted. "Sophie, look!"

chapter 9

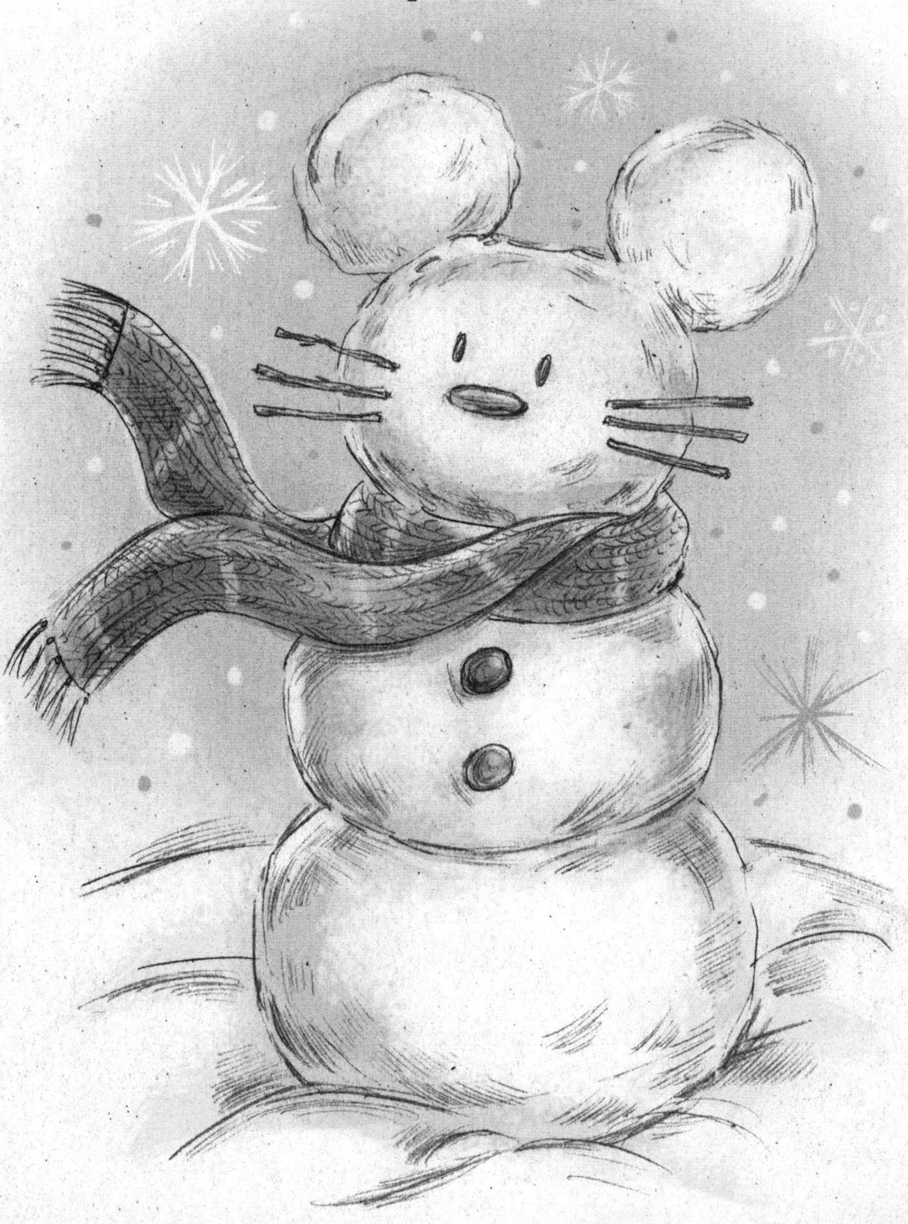

ROCK-a-Bye, Pippa

Sophie ran up over the crest of the hill. There, set back from the slope, stood the snow mouse. And around its neck was a beautiful purple scarf!

"My scarf!" Sophie cried. "Of course! I was adding the finishing touches. I wanted to see how my scarf looked on the snow mouse. But then Owen hit me with a snowball!

And I got swept up in our snowball fight!"

Owen blushed. "Sorry," he said.

Sophie smiled. "No, it's not your fault." She took the scarf and wrapped it around her neck. It was a little icy from being left on the hilltop. But Sophie didn't care. "We found it!" she cheered.

Her friends cheered with her.

Then Owen shivered. "I think it's time for me to go home," he said.

Hattie nodded. "Me too. I could use a hot chocolate."

That sounded good to Sophie. Her toes *were* starting to get chilly. So she and Hattie and Owen walked Pippa home. They stood outside the doorway of the nest.

"Bye, Pippa!" said Owen.

Hattie smiled. "I'm really glad we met you!"

Sophie waved good-bye. "Are you going to go back to sleep now?" she asked.

Pippa stared back at them with big eyes.

Big, wide-open, wide-awake eyes.

"I *should* go back to sleep," Pippa replied. "But I don't feel so sleepy. . . . "

"Oh," said Sophie. She looked at Hattie and Owen. "Well, maybe we could stay a while longer?"

Hattie and Owen understood. "We need to help Pippa fall asleep again!" Hattie said.

Pippa smiled. "Would you?" she said. "Thank you!"

Sophie thought for a second. "How about a lullaby?" she suggested.

Pippa nodded. She snuggled down and closed her eyes. Sophie began to sing. It was a lullaby that her dad loved about a sleepy squirrel.

She sang the whole song twice. Pippa's eyes were still closed. "Did it work?" Sophie whispered to Hattie.

Pippa's eyes popped open. "Nope," she said.

Hattie yawned. "It made *me* sleepy," she said.

Seeing Hattie yawn made Owen yawn. Then Sophie yawned too. The only one not yawning was Pippa.

Owen spoke up. "My mom rocked me to sleep when I was little," he said.

"Too bad we don't have a rocking chair," Hattie pointed out.

They thought it over. "I have an idea!" Pippa said suddenly. "Wait here." She tiptoed inside the nest. When she came out, she had a blanket. "We could make a hammock!"

"Yes!" cried Sophie. She tied one end of the blanket to a branch. Hattie tied the other end to another branch.

Pippa climbed in and closed her eyes. Sophie, Hattie, and Owen rocked the hammock gently. Side to side. Side to side . . .

They rocked her for a long while.

But then Pippa opened one eye. "Sorry," she said. "It's not working."

Pippa climbed out of the hammock. She plopped down on the ground. "It's no use," she said. "You guys should go home. I'm sure I'll get sleepy . . . sometime."

Sophie frowned. They couldn't just leave Pippa. But what could they do? How could they help her fall asleep?

chapter 10

Good Night, Sleep Tight

Sophie sat down next to Pippa. Hattie and Owen did too. They were out of ideas. So they decided to just keep Pippa company for a bit.

"It was a good snow day," said Hattie. "Wasn't it?"

Pippa nodded. "I never knew winter could be so much fun!"

They took turns talking about

which activity they liked best. "Sledding was my favorite," said Owen. "Our sled track was really fast!"

Hattie went next. "My favorite part was snow hide-and-seek." She was really proud of her hiding place. "But I also loved the imprints we made in the snow!"

Sophie thought it over. "It *is* hard to pick just one thing I liked best. Let's see. . . ." She listed *everything* they had done. She noted what was fun about each. She gave each a score from one to ten. When she was done, all the scores were the same: ten. "Nope," Sophie said. "I can't pick. How about you, Pippa?"

"Huh?" Pippa mumbled. Her eyelids looked heavy. Then she yawned a huge yawn.

"Oh!" said Hattie, jumping up. "I think someone is ready for bed now."

Sophie and Owen jumped up too. They helped Pippa to her feet. She swayed sleepily, then shuffled into the nest.

"See you in the springtime," Sophie

whispered as Pippa disappeared.

They waited outside for a minute, listening. But there wasn't a sound from inside the nest. Owen shrugged. "That's a good sign," he said.

Then there was one very loud snore.

Sophie giggled. "That's an even better sign!"

Sophie got home just as her dad was pouring the hot cocoa. Before dinner, she went up to her room. She got out her brushes and paints. She

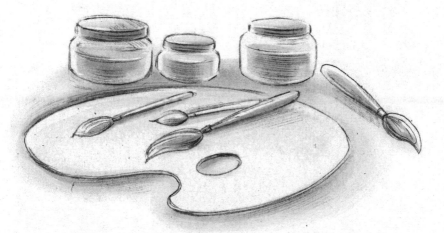

mixed some white with a touch of blue. Then Sophie painted a snowy scene at Hickory Hill.

Later, at bedtime, she snuggled into her warm, cozy bed. *Time for my long winter's sleep,* Sophie thought.

But not as long as Pippa's! Tomorrow's another snow day!

The End

Here's a peek at the next
Adventures of Sophie Mouse book!

Mrs. Wise closed the book she had just read out loud to the class. Sophie sighed. *Wow! What a story!* she thought.

A groundhog had found a hidden stairway in a tree. He'd climbed it all the way to the top branch. But the stairway kept going. So the ground-hog did too—into the clouds and over a rainbow! He'd found a magical world on the other side.

Sophie loved the story and the way it was told. It didn't feel like a fairy tale. It was written as if it had really happened!

"All right class," said Mrs. Wise. "Who can tell me what a legend is?"

Lydie, Hattie Frog's big sister, raised her hand.

"It's a story that animals believe in," Lydie said. "But there's no proof that it really happened."

the adventures of
SOPHiE MOUSE

For excerpts, activities, and more about
these adorable tales & tails, visit
AdventuresofSophieMouse.com!